Disney Junior

PUPPY DOG PALS

5 minute stories

DISNEP PRESS
Los Angeles • New York

For information address Disney Press, 1200 Grand Central Avenue, Glendale, California 91201.

Printed in the United States of America

First Hardcover Edition, September 2019

Library of Congress Control Number: 2019938813

1 3 5 7 9 10 8 6 4 2

ISBN 978-1-368-04700-5

FAC-038091-19221

For more Disney Press fun, visit www.disneybooks.com

CONTENTS

meet A.R.F.

"Are you ready for liftoff, Rolly?" Bingo asks his brother.

"Just gotta put on my safety gear," Rolly replies.

Bingo gets a running start and jumps onto a chair. The footrest pops out and launches Rolly like a rocket.

"I'm flying!" Rolly shouts. "Wait. Now I'm falling!"

Rolly lands on the couch and collapses in giggles.

Just then, their owner, Bob, comes home with a surprise. "Check out what I made for you!"

Bingo and Rolly examine the surprise. It looks like a dog, but . . . it is not soft and furry. It does not have a wet nose and floppy ears. It does not return Bingo's and Rolly's "Hello, nice to meet you" sniffs.

"I call him Auto-doggie Robotic Friend, or A.R.F.," says Bob.

Bingo and Rolly do not know what to think of their new housemate.

"A.R.F. is here to do it all," Bob says. "I even programmed him to clean up any mess that you make before I get home so we can have more time to play!"

After Bob leaves for work, Bingo asks, "What are we supposed to do with you?"

"Whatever you do on a regular day," A.R.F. answers robotically.

"Well, some days we go on fun adventures," Rolly says. "And other days we stay here and make a really BIG mess!"

A.R.F. gets excited. He would *love* to clean up after Bingo and Rolly's messes!

Bingo and Rolly
get right to work.

Normally, when Bob
comes home to that kind
of mess, it takes him a long
time to clean up—time that
he could spend playing
with the puppies. But
today is different.

"A.R.F. loves to
clean!" says A.R.F.
"Look at that
Auto-doggie Robotic
Friend go!" Bingo
shouts as he wags
his tail.

The puppies are all tuckered out from their mess-making. They curl up together for a nap.

"What will A.R.F. do now?" A.R.F. wonders aloud. Then he spots a piece of kibble stuck to Hissy's fur—more mess to clean!

A.R.F. wheels toward Hissy. She leaps around the living room, trying to get away from A.R.F. "Sorry! Running away from dogs is just something cats do!" she says.

A.R.F. does not give up. He chases Hissy all around the house. But now the house is an even bigger mess than before!

Bingo and Rolly wake up and see the new mess.

"How come you're not cleaning it up?" Rolly asks A.R.F.

"Bob only programmed A.R.F. to clean up after Bingo and Rolly, not Hissy and A.R.F.," A.R.F. says.

"I guess that means we have a mission," Bingo says. "Mission: clean up the house!"

"Let's get this mess up off the floor!" Rolly says.

The pups work as fast as they can to get everything back to how it was.

"Just gotta wash these towels and our job is done!" exclaims Bingo.

"You can never have too much soap," Rolly adds.

While the puppies go to the backyard to play, the washing machine starts to overflow. Soon the laundry room is filled with soap bubbles!

In the doghouse, Rolly plays a doggie video game while Bingo runs on a doggie treadmill.

Suddenly, an alarm goes off—Bob is almost home! The puppies race back inside.

As soon as Bingo and Rolly run into the house, they slip on the soapy floor! "Whoaaaa!" they shout as they slide across the kitchen.

"How much soap did you put in that washing machine?" Hissy wants to know.

"Um, all of it," Bingo tells her. "We need to turn it off before things get even soapier and sudsier!"

But when they open the door to the laundry room, a huge wall of soapy bubbles crashes all over them.

"Tidal wave!" shouts Rolly.

"Hang pup!" says Bingo as they surf the wave of bubbles.

Bingo, Rolly, and Hissy all run to the top of the stairs to escape the bubbles that are filling the whole house!

"The soapsuds keep getting higher, but there's nowhere else to go!" Bingo says.

"Back, soapsuds, get back!" Hissy hisses as she swipes at the bubbles.

Suddenly, A.R.F. appears from inside the bubbles. "Don't worry! A.R.F. will clean up Bingo and Rolly's bubbly mess!" A.R.F. uses his vacuum to suck up all the bubbles in the house.

"All right, A.R.F.!" Rolly shouts.

After the very last bubble disappears, Bob walks in the door.
"Wow, look how sparkly clean this place is!" he says. "I guess my new
invention really worked. Now we have more time to play!"

Bob is happy the house is clean. A.R.F. is happy that Bob is happy.
And Bingo and Rolly are happiest when they are playing with Bob.
MISSION ACCOMPLISHED!

Hawaii Pug-O

"**S**urf's up, Rolly!" says Bingo, racing through the house on his doggie skateboard.

"Bow to the wow, Bingo! I'm right on your tail!" Rolly calls.

Suddenly, their boards catch on the rug, sending the brothers flying through the air . . . and into their owner's bed.

"I'm awake! I'm awake!" Bob says, sitting up. "Now there are two little fellas I like seeing early in the morning!"

At breakfast, Bob sees a newspaper ad about Hawaii.

"Big waves, sandy beaches," he says dreamily. "I sure would love to feel the sand between my toes."

But Bob can't go to Hawaii today. He has to go to work.

As soon as Bob leaves, Bingo turns to Rolly. "We have a mission! We need to go to Hawaii to get sand for Bob's toes!"

"'Cause happy toes means happy Bob!" says Rolly. "Mission: get Hawaiian sand for Bob's toes!"

They run to the doghouse to get ready for their mission. One of Bob's inventions puts special collars on the pups and then fills compartments in the collars with dog treats!

Rolly tosses an old sock into another compartment.

"I always feel better carrying an old sock," says Rolly.

"Who doesn't?" Bingo agrees.

They are ready to roll! The pups race to the airport. They find Frank and Esther heading to Hawaii.

When the pups land, they run down the steps, excited for the next part of their mission. First stop: the beach!

A hop, a skip, and a jump later, Bingo and Rolly arrive.

"Look at all this sand!" says Bingo. "It's perfect for Bob's toes!"

But Rolly is not thinking about Bob. He's thinking about catching a sand crab.

"Where did that crabby crab go?" Rolly says.

He digs and digs, looking for the crab. Rolly kicks up so much sand that Bingo gets buried!

"Now we just have to get this sand home," says Bingo. "We need something big that flies. Let's get to work."

Bingo and Rolly decide to make their own airplane—out of sand!

"Now we can fly all this sand back to Bob!" Rolly exclaims.

"Let's go!" says Bingo.

Rolly's eyes get wide. "Wave!"

"Right! Let's wave goodbye to everyone," Bingo agrees.

"No!" Rolly says, pointing to the ocean. "WAVE!"

With the airplane gone, the puppies decide they need a boat instead. They build one out of sand. But before they can set sail, another wave crashes over them!

Rolly says, "Sorry to abandon ship, but I've got a crab to catch!"

"We came to get sand for Bob, so why are you walking away?" Bingo asks.

"I'm not. You are!" Rolly replies.

But neither of the puppies is walking anywhere. . . . They're floating away!

Just then, a dog on a surfboard floats by. "Aloha, puppy dudes! You here for the surfing contest?" he asks.

"We've never surfed for real before," Rolly says.

"It's just like riding our skateboards!" says Bingo confidently. "Hang pup!"

Bingo and Rolly ride a wave to shore, howling for joy the whole way. When they reach the beach, a trophy is waiting for them. They won the surfing contest!

Rolly shrugs. "We must've gotten bonus points for being extra huggable."

"This trophy's cool," says Bingo, "but we still need to bring back sand for Bob's toes."

But Rolly's mind is not on their mission—it's on catching that pesky crab. "I'm going to find you, Crabby!"

Rolly starts to dig, sending sand flying through the air—and into the trophy.

"Hey, this is the perfect way to get the sand back to Bob," Bingo says. "Keep digging!"

"Anything for you, Brother!" Rolly says, digging faster and faster until the trophy is full.

The pups take the trophy full of sand back home. They're about to
go into the house when the gardener walks by with a leaf blower. He
accidentally blows all the sand away!

"It's gone. All of it," Bingo says sadly.

"Except for the sand that's still in my ears," says Rolly.

"Yeah," Bingo agrees. "We really got covered in that stuff!"

The puppies scratch and shake, sending the sand flying.

Suddenly, Bingo gets an idea!

The puppies run inside to wait for Bob to come home from work.

"Hey, guys!" Bob says happily as he walks in the door. "I've been looking forward to seeing you all day."

Bingo and Rolly look at each other, nod, and then shake, shake, shake!

Bob starts laughing. "How in the world did you two get so sandy?"

"Now there's sand everywhere—even between my toes!" says Bob.
"But you know, that feels pretty good." He wiggles his toes and smiles.
"Must be how the beach in Hawaii would feel."

Bingo and Rolly look at each other and smile.

MISSION ACCOMPLISHED!

DESIGN-a-DOG

Bingo and Rolly are curled up on the couch, watching their favorite show. "*Captain Dog* will be back after these messages," says the announcer.

"How would you like to build your own stuffed animal, dress it up, and take it home to play?" the lady in the commercial says.

"I would *love* that!" Bingo declares.

The puppies sing along to the ad: "Come to Design-a-Dog today!"

Later that day, Bob walks downstairs, carrying a box of old toys. "I had tons of fun with these toys, but it's time someone else got to have fun with them," he says. Bob sets down the box and heads to work.

A box full of toys? Bingo and Rolly cannot wait to see what's inside!

The first thing the puppies find is a worn old stuffed dog.

"I like this thing!" says Rolly. "It's shakity-shaky!"

Bingo wants to shake it, too. The puppies each grab one end of the toy and shake. Suddenly . . . *RIIIP!* Stuffing flies everywhere!

"You just ruined Ruff-Ruff!" Hissy exclaims. "He was Bob's favorite toy when he was a kid."

"Then it's our mission to fix him," Bingo says. "I know where to go!"

The puppies rush to their doghouse for their special collars and then head out for Mission: fix Ruff-Ruff.

Bingo and Rolly take Ruff-Ruff to Design-a-Dog. The store is filled with stuffed dogs of every size, shape, and color. Three big machines make sure each toy is stuffed, sewn, and groomed. Bingo and Rolly spot the lady from the commercial talking to some children.

"Follow those kids!" Rolly says.

They follow the kids to the stuffing machine. Once the kids walk away, the puppies hop inside the machine. They hook up the stuffing hose to fill Ruff-Ruff till he's a perfectly poufy pooch.

Ruff-Ruff gets stuffed with more and more fluff until . . . the hose comes loose!

"Stuffing storm!" the puppies shout excitedly.

Next they head to the sewing machine.

Chloe sits down and powers the sewing machine by pressing the pedals with her feet. "This is fun!" she says, giggling.

When the kids move on, the puppies put Ruff-Ruff inside the sewing machine and jump onto the pedals.

Bingo says, "When I go up, up, up, you go—"

"Down, down, down!" Rolly shouts as they sew Ruff-Ruff.

The last stop is the grooming machine. "First we get the doggies clean," the lady explains. "Then we give them some style, and then some bling!"

"Let's get Ruff-Ruff cleaned, styled, and blinged before we take him back to Bob," says Bingo. "And we might as well get ourselves looking good, too!"

The puppies leap into the grooming machine with Ruff-Ruff. Brushes and blow-dryers clean, style, and bling up Ruff-Ruff and the pups.

"We did it!" Bingo says. "Ruff-Ruff looks better than ever!"
"And we look pretty pup-tacular ourselves," declares Rolly.

The pups are ready to get Ruff-Ruff home when they see the lady heading toward them. "It's time for a tea-pup party!" she says. The kids scurry over to choose a toy to play with.

"This one is my favorite," Chloe says, picking up Ruff-Ruff.

"I want two," says another girl, grabbing Bingo and Rolly.

The pups don't know what to do—so they freeze! The girl dresses them in costumes and makes them drink pretend tea.

"There's nothing in the cup," Rolly whispers to Bingo. "I'm still thirsty!"

Next it's time for the Design-a-Dog roller-skating sing along.

"Whoaaaa!" Rolly calls, slipping and sliding on his skates.

Finally, it's time for the kids to pick out toy puppies to take home. Chloe is just about to choose Ruff-Ruff!

"We need to grab Ruff-Ruff and get out of here!" Bingo says.

Bingo and Rolly skate toward the pile of toy puppies as fast as they can.

Suddenly, Rolly loses control and slides into a display with a crash!
Chloe turns around, giving Bingo just enough time to jump into the pile
of toys, grab Ruff-Ruff, and go!

Back home at last, Bingo and Rolly show off Ruff-Ruff's makeover.

"This thing looks amazing!" says Hissy.

"Yup! Bob won't even know we took it out of the box," Bingo says.

Just then, Bob walks in the front door. After he greets his pets, he takes the box of toys outside for the donation center to pick up.

As Bob sets down the box, Chloe and her mom walk by.

"That looks like the doggie from the store!" Chloe exclaims.

"How would you like to keep him?" Bob asks with a smile.

Rolly turns to Bingo. "Bob is happy and so is Chloe! High paw!"

MISSION ACCOMPLISHED!

HISSY'S BIG DAY

It is a perfect day for a walk in the backyard.

"Let's see if we can go even faster!" Bingo says as he presses a button. *Zoom!* The treadmill speeds up.

"This is so much fun!" Rolly says.

"This is absolutely horrible!" Hissy shouts.

Bingo stops the treadmill. "What's wrong?" he asks.

"Everything! I woke up too early and couldn't get back to sleep. I broke a nail on my scratching post. And then this happened!" Hissy puts her favorite toy down in front of them. "Runny the Bunny stopped running."

All Hissy wants to do is take a nap in her favorite shady spot, but the treadmill is in the way.

"You can still nap there if you want," Rolly tells her.

Hissy lies down on the treadmill, but when she stretches, she accidentally turns it on. "WHOOOA!"

"Hey! Wait! Slow down!" Hissy says as she tries to turn the treadmill off. But she hits the wrong button and it goes even faster! Hissy is thrown off the treadmill with a thud. "This no-good day just got even more no good."

Bob hears the commotion and walks outside. "It looks like you've had a really tough morning," he says, picking Hissy up. "And Runny the Bunny is broken, too?"

Hissy responds with a miserable meow.

Bob tells Bingo and Rolly, "Try to be good puppy brothers to your kitty sister while I'm at work, okay?"

"Did you hear that, Rolly?" Bingo asks. "Bob asked us to take care of Hissy."

"We always have fun on our missions. We should take her on one," Rolly replies. "Wait, do we have a mission?"

"We do now!" Bingo exclaims. "Mission: make sure Hissy has the BEST DAY EVER!"

Bingo and Rolly tell Hissy they are taking her to a surprise place.

"You brought me to the dog park?" Hissy says.

"It's a place that we love, and we figured you'd love it, too!" Bingo says.

Hissy doesn't think she'll love the dog park, but she's willing to give it a try. She decides to let Bingo and Rolly play with their puppy friends while she explores.

But it isn't long before Hissy runs into Cupcake, the neighborhood bully, and her sidekick, Rufus. Cupcake commands Rufus to chase Hissy through the park. Soon other dogs in the park join the chase!

Bingo and Rolly have to help her hide . . . and fast.

Cupcake sees them and asks, "Did you guys see a cat?"

"If we did, we don't see one now," Bingo replies.

"Maybe she went that way!" Cupcake says. She and the other dogs run off in the opposite direction.

The pups continue on their mission to cheer up their sister.

"I guess the dog park wasn't the best place to take a cat," Bingo says.
"But we think you'll like this place!"

"The pet store is perfect for hide-and-seek!" Rolly adds.

"Give us a minute to hide and then come find us," Bingo tells Hissy.

"I might give you more than a minute," Hissy says. "Like however
many minutes I spend taking a good long nap."

"I found a perfect
place to hide!" Rolly says.

"Me too!" says Bingo.

Hissy finds the perfect
place to take a nap: a cozy
bed on a high shelf.

Later on, Frank and Esther enter the pet shop, looking for something for their pet iguana, Iggy. Frank picks up the bed where Hissy is sleeping, but he doesn't see her in it. He turns it upside down to look at the price tag, and Hissy falls right out.

Luckily, cats always land on their feet!

Meanwhile, Bingo and Rolly think their hiding spots are too good for Hissy to ever find them. They decide to look for her instead.

"Rolly and I have one more place to take you," Bingo says excitedly when they find her in an aisle.

The last surprise location is the small train in the park.

"Don't you just love feeling the wind on your face and the sun on your fur?" Bingo asks Hissy.

Hissy dodges the doggie drool coming from Bingo's and Rolly's slobbery tongues. "It's a lot wetter than I thought it would be," she replies.

Hissy hops to a different seat to avoid her brothers' slobber. She
tries to relax and looks out at the view. She's even starting to enjoy
the breeze until . . . the train whistle startles her and she falls off!
"I just want to go home before this day gets any worse."

There is just one problem with that plan: Hissy stepped on bubble gum, and her paw is stuck to the tracks. She looks up and realizes the train is coming right toward her! "This day just got worse!" she howls.

Bingo and Rolly leap into action.

"We're gonna have to save her with Bingo and Rolly power!" Rolly shouts.

Rolly pushes while Bingo pulls, and they free Hissy in the nick of time.

Back home, Hissy lies in her favorite shady spot in the backyard. "I guess this day didn't end up like we wanted it to for Hissy," Bingo says sadly.

"It started bad and just kept getting more and more bad after that," Rolly says.

"It wasn't *all* bad," Hissy says with a smile. "I found out I can run faster than those dogs. And I got a pretty good nap at the pet store. And the best part was, whenever I got into trouble, the two of you rescued me—which made me feel kinda special."

Just then, Bob comes home with a surprise. "Hissy, this will cheer you up!"

It's Runny the Bunny. Bob fixed it!

"There's no way you can catch it before I do," Hissy tells the puppies. "But I'd like to see you try!" The three of them laugh and giggle as they race after the toy.

MISSION ACCOMPLISHED!

THE LaST PUP-iCORN

Keia is the new puppy in town. She just moved in next door to Bingo and Rolly. Keia loves her owner Chloe more than anything in the world!

Chloe has something special for Keia: a tiny unicorn costume.

"There, now you're my pup-icorn!" Chloe says. "My mom got me this because she knows how much I wish I had a unicorn."

Keia wags her tail. "I wish you had a unicorn, too!"

Chloe waves goodbye and leaves for school.

"I wish I could do something special for Chloe like you do for Bob," says Keia.

"Keia, I've got an idea!" Bingo says. "We can go on a mission!"

"That sounds amazing!" Keia replies. "If Chloe wants a unicorn, then I'm going on a mission to get her one. Where do we find a unicorn?"

Bingo and Rolly know that A.R.F. always knows.

"A.R.F. does not know where to find a unicorn," A.R.F. tells them. "But A.R.F. does know that the unicorn of the sea lives deep in the cold, cold Arctic Ocean."

"Find a sea unicorn in the Arctic Ocean," Rolly says. "How hard can that be?"

"Chloe will LOVE it!" says Keia, wagging her tail.

The three puppies keep a lookout from the deck of the ship.

When Rolly sees a horn pop out of the water, he shouts, "Sea unicorn over there!"

They activate their scuba gear.

"PUP-ICORN AWAAAAY!" Keia shouts as she dives into the cold, cold Arctic Ocean.

The puppies look and look and look.

They don't see a sea unicorn anywhere!

"Maybe that whale can help us," Keia suggests. "Um, Mr. Whale?"

When the whale turns around, Keia gasps as she sees his giant horn. "You're the sea unicorn!" she squeals.

"Actually, I'm a narwhal," the whale explains. "I'm just called the unicorn of the sea because of my horn. Fun fact—it's really a tooth!"

"I bet he uses a lot of toothpaste," Rolly whispers to his brother.

"Come to think of it, the unicorn on Chloe's sweater did look a lot more like a horse than a whale," Keia admits.

"Perhaps a horse might know more about unicorns than I do," the narwhal says.

"Thank you, Mr. Sea Unicorn!" Keia calls. "I mean, Mr. Narwhal!"

"Don't forget to floss!" Rolly adds.

Bingo, Rolly, and Keia head back home and run straight to the park.
"Horses!" Keia yells.

Bingo and Rolly greet their friend Betty. "Do you know where to
find a unicorn?" Rolly asks her.

Betty has never seen a unicorn. But her friend Bea points to the
other side of the park, where the Medieval Faire is going on. Keia gasps
in awe when she sees the magical creature in the distance.

Then she takes off running. "I'M SO EXCITED!"

Bingo and Rolly race after Keia through the Medieval Faire.

"Mr. Unicorn, Mr. Unicorn!" Keia calls.

"You may call me Reginald, m'lady," the unicorn replies.

"Would you come to my house to be Chloe's unicorn, please?" Keia asks him. "She loves, loves, LOVES unicorns!"

Reginald tells Keia that he would be honored to meet Chloe. "Hop aboard," he says. "Tallyho, puppy pals!"

Reginald rears.

He shakes his flowing mane.

And then . . .

Reginald's horn and mane fall to the ground!

"You're not a unicorn, either?" Keia asks sadly.

"Alas, I'm merely a humble horse pretending to be a unicorn,"
Reginald explains. "I don't think anyone's ever seen a *real* unicorn."

Keia walks away, heartbroken. If no one has ever seen a unicorn, she will never find one for Chloe.

"You know, Keia," Bingo says. "With or without a unicorn, you'll always be perfect for Chloe. She's your person, and you're her puppy."

"You do give Chloe the best puppy licks," Rolly points out.

"And you make the best things out of sticks," Bingo adds.

"That's it!" Keia shouts.

Keia runs to the craft table at the Faire. She grabs a few short sticks, a few long ones, and one pointy, horn-shaped stick. Then she gets to work.

"Now Chloe can have her unicorn!" Keia says.

"PUP-TASTIC!" Rolly cheers.

When Chloe gets home from school, she sees the unicorn Keia made for her. She loves it!

But not nearly as much as she loves her puppy.

MISSION ACCOMPLISHED!

THE FRENCH TOAST CONNECTION

"Breakfast is one of my favorite meals of the day," Bingo tells his brother.

"It's tied for first with lunch and dinner!" Rolly mumbles with his mouth full.

"Good morning, pup-stars," Bob says as he walks downstairs. "It's time for my breakfast, too. I'm going to have my favorite: French toast!"

"Oh, no!" Bob says. "I don't have any bread for my French toast! Argghh!" Bob lets out a sigh. "Sorry, guys," he tells the pups as he leaves for work. "I get as grumpy as a bear if I don't have French toast. Hope I feel better later tonight."

After Bob leaves, Bingo turns to Rolly. "Did you hear that? Bob said he gets as grumpy as a bear if he doesn't have French toast!"

"I don't want Bob being a bear, I want Bob being a Bob!" Rolly says.

Bingo and Rolly run outside to the doghouse and collar up.

Mission: get bread for French toast! And the best place for French bread is . . .

FRANCE!

"We have to bring home the best kind of French-toast-makin' bread for Bob," Bingo says when they arrive.

"But where are we going to find it?" Rolly asks.

Just then, the pups overhear Frank and Esther talking about a bakery with the best French bread in Paris.

Bingo and Rolly follow the couple to the bakery. But when they get there, they find out all the bread has been stolen!

"Why is everyone so worried about French bread?" a nearby pigeon asks. "Now, if it was birdseed, I'd understand. We pigeons love that stuff!"

"Are there any clues that might tell us who took the bread?" a detective asks the baker.

"I saw tiny footprints leading away from where the bread used to be," the baker responds.

"We need to find someone with tiny feet!" Rolly says.
The puppies look around them and see all kinds of feet—

big feet,

medium feet,

silly feet—

but no tiny feet. Until . . .

They spot mice on the street!

"Those tiny feet would have left tiny footprints!" shouts Bingo.

"Stop in the name of the paws!"

The mice take off in a panic, running and squeaking.

"Those tiny feet move those tiny bodies fast!" Rolly says.

Bingo and Rolly chase the mice all through the city.

"If those mice get away, we'll never find out who took the bread, and Bob won't get his French toast!" says Rolly.

"Excuse us—puppies coming through!" Bingo calls. "We've got a mystery to solve."

Finally, the puppies corner the mice in an alley. "We've got you now, bread takers!" Bingo says triumphantly.

"We did not take any bread," a mouse tells them.

"Then why were you running away?" asks Bingo.

"Because we were being chased by two scary-looking dogs!" the mouse replies.

The puppies return to the scene of the stolen bread.

"If only there were more clues to follow," the detective tells the baker.

But there are! The puppies spot a trail of bread crumbs leading away from the bakery.

"Follow the trail of bread crumbs!" Bingo shouts.

"It will lead us to who took the bread!" Rolly says as they run. Bingo and Rolly follow the trail all through the city.

They find bread crumbs in front of the Arc de Triomphe . . .

and the Louvre Museum . . .

and Notre-Dame Cathedral.

The trail leads them all the way to the Eiffel Tower. "Race ya to the top," Bingo says as he runs up the stairs.

"The race is *on*!" replies Rolly.

When the puppies do some more sniffing, they discover dozens of loaves of French bread hidden all over the Eiffel Tower. But where are the tiny-footed bread burglars?

"Maybe we should ask those pigeons if they know who is hiding that bread," Rolly says.

"WHOA!" one pigeon says to the pups. "You caught us *bread*-handed!"

The pigeons apologize for stealing the bread. "People kept feeding us bread, but we just wanted birdseed!" one of the pigeons explains.

"You could just not eat the bread," Rolly suggests.

"And then people would feed you birdseed instead," Bingo adds.

"That is one really good idea!" the pigeon replies.

Now that the pigeons have agreed to stop stealing bread, the baker has plenty of it for everyone.

"You cute puppies look like you want some bread," he says to Bingo and Rolly. He hands them a loaf of delicious French bread.

When Bob gets home from work, he is overjoyed to see fresh French bread on the kitchen counter for his French toast.

"Bob is happy with his French toast!" Bingo says.

Rolly giggles. "And *I'm* happy he won't turn into a bear."

MISSION ACCOMPLISHED!

ONE SMALL RUFF FOR PUP-KIND

It's a bright, sunny day, and Bingo, Rolly, and Keia are playing together at Chloe's house.

"Ground control to Major A.R.F.!" Bingo calls.

"We're ready for blastoff!" says Rolly.

A.R.F. looks back at the puppies and says, "Let's do this!" A.R.F. speeds around the yard, pulling the puppies in a wagon behind him.

Just then, Chloe runs into the backyard, followed by her parents.

A.R.F. screeches to a halt, and the puppies all topple into a puppy pile at Chloe's feet.

Bob hears the commotion and looks over the fence. "Hiya, neighbors! I hope those puppies aren't causing too much trouble."

"No way, Mr. Bob," Chloe says, picking up her puppy. "I just wanted to give Keia a cuddle before I go to Astronaut Summer Camp!"

"Astronaut Summer Camp? Fun!" Bob says.

"Yeah, I'm gonna learn all about outer space," Chloe explains. "I may even touch a moon rock!"

"I've always dreamed of having a real moon rock for my rock collection!" Bob says. "Well, gotta head to work. Have a great time at camp!"

"We'd better go, sweetie," says Chloe's mom.

"I wish I could bring you all with me," Chloe says to the puppies. "But at least I'll have Ruff-Ruff to help me fall asleep at bedtime."

"I hope Chloe has the best time ever," says Keia once Chloe leaves. "Right, Ruff-Ruff? Oh, no! Chloe must have dropped him by accident!"

"We gotta get Ruff-Ruff back to Chloe," says Bingo.

Rolly jumps to his feet. "Sounds like we have an astro-pup mission!"

The pups pile into A.R.F.'s sidecar, activate their helmets, and are soon on their way to Astronaut Summer Camp!

When they arrive, they bump right into a model Mars robot. His name is Rover.

"We're trying to find Chloe so she can have Ruff-Ruff by bedtime," Bingo explains. "But this place is so big we don't know where to start."

Rover beeps and wags his tail excitedly.

"Rover knows exactly where to start," A.R.F. translates.

Rover leads them to a map of the whole camp.

"Wow, this place is humongous!" Rolly exclaims.

"Yeah," agrees Bingo, "we've got a lot of places to check."

A.R.F. takes a picture of the map so they can have it with them in case they get lost.

"Thanks, A.R.F.!" says Bingo. "Now let's get looking!"

First the puppies look for Chloe in the space exhibit hall . . . but Chloe isn't there.

Then the pups climb up to the high-g training centrifuge . . . but Chloe isn't there, either.

Next the puppies walk up a ramp and board a rocket . . . but still no Chloe.

"Don't worry, Keia. We'll find her," Rolly says. He pats Keia on the back and accidentally stumbles, bumping into a button.

Suddenly, the hydraulic door closes!

"A.R.F. will open the door," A.R.F. says. He goes to press a big blue button in the control room. Rover tries to stop him, but it's too late: the rocket begins to shake!

"*Automatic space rocket launch initiated,*" announces an intercom voice. "*Please put on your space suits.*" The intercom voice initiates the countdown: "*Three, two, one . . . blastoff!*"

Rover beeps and bleeps. He has good news and bad news.

A.R.F. translates: "The good news is that this is an automatic rocket, so we will be going back to Astronaut Summer Camp. . . . But the rocket will take us to the moon first."

"Let's go!" the puppies exclaim.

The rocket soon lands safely on the moon. A.R.F. presses a button to take them back to Earth . . . but it's the wrong button again!

This time the button activates the hydraulic door, and all the air gets sucked out as the door opens. Ruff-Ruff isn't buckled in and flies out the door and onto the moon!

The puppies tumble out of the rocket ship onto the moon's surface, bouncing and spinning in the low gravity, looking for Ruff-Ruff.

"That's one small step for a puppy," says Bingo, "and one giant leap for pup-kind!"

"Hey, look!" Rolly shouts. "A moon rock for Bob!" He quickly grabs it and puts it in his collar to take home.

Keia spots Ruff-Ruff bouncing into a crater a short distance away. Before long, they manage to get him safely back to the rocket ship— and buckled in.

"We got Ruff-Ruff!" cheers Bingo.

"Please take us home, Major A.R.F.," Rolly says.

This time, A.R.F. asks Rover which button is the right one to push. Soon they are headed back to Earth and, more important, back to find Chloe.

As soon as the rocket lands, the pups rush out. The campers are all headed to their bunks for bedtime.

"The bunks are here," A.R.F. says, pointing out the exact location on the map. "But A.R.F. got a little hurt on the moon, so A.R.F. asked Rover to help get you there."

Rover and the puppies speed through the exhibit hall, turn left past the high-g machine, and head straight for Chloe's bunk!

Inside the cabin, Keia spots Chloe's backpack. "There you go, Ruff-Ruff," she says, tucking him inside it. "Now you can help Chloe sleep. That's *your* mission."

"Now let's get back to A.R.F.!" says Rolly.

As soon as they find A.R.F., Rover fixes his faulty circuit.

"A.R.F. feels better!" A.R.F. says. "And now A.R.F. must take everyone home."

The puppies climb aboard and wave goodbye to their new friend.

Bingo and Rolly make it home in time to greet Bob when he gets back from work. Rolly activates his collar, and the moon rock falls out.

"Wow!" Bob says, picking it up. "It almost looks like a moon rock." The puppies look at each other and smile.

"It'll be perfect for my collection!" Bob says. "But not as perfect as coming home to my two favorite pups."

MISSION ACCOMPLISHED!

ADVENTURES IN PUPPY-SITTING

One morning, Bob wakes the puppies with some good news. "Morning, sleepy-snouts! Guess what, guys? My friend just got a new puppy named Baby."

Baby? Bingo and Rolly think that's a funny name for a puppy!

"She doesn't want the puppy to get lonely while she's at work, so I said Baby can stay here with you today, and you can keep her company!"

The pups think that is a great idea!

As soon as Bob leaves to get Baby, Bingo looks at Rolly. "Let's get ready!" Their mission: to be the best puppy-sitters ever!

"Let's give Baby her own dish. You know, to help her feel at home," Rolly suggests.

Bingo finds a small teacup to use as Baby's bowl. "If we each share a few of our kibbles, that'll fill it up."

Rolly looks at his brother. "What else do great puppy-sitters do?"

"They're good at making sure puppies get naps," Bingo says. "We need to find a spot for Baby's nap time."

From the bookshelf, Hissy chimes in. "Baby could sleep in one of Bob's shoes. That's what you two goofballs used to do."

Rolly smiles as he remembers sleeping in Loafy, Bob's old loafer shoe. The puppies go searching for it in Bob's closet.

Next they decide to gather some toys for Baby to play with. Rolly wonders what kind of toys little puppies like.

Hissy looks down at them. "Okay, first of all, you're still puppies."

Rolly shakes his head. "We mean when we were *littler* puppies. We get a little bit less little every day."

Hissy points out a photo. "Well, you loved that squeaky toy. I used to throw it for you to fetch when I was bored."

Bingo's eyes grow wide. "You mean Mr. Mousey? I haven't seen that toy in forever!" The pups run to find Mr. Mousey. They know Baby will love it, too.

Just then, the pups hear the front door open. They run over, excited to meet little Baby. But when the new puppy walks through the door, Bingo, Rolly, and Hissy are in for a great big surprise. Little Baby is a gigantic Great Dane puppy!

Bingo looks up—*way* up—at the new arrival. "Whoa. That's one big baby."

Rolly shakes his head. "She is *not* going to fit in that shoe."

After Bob leaves for work, Baby starts whimpering and crying. But Bingo and Rolly know just what to do to make the puppy feel better.

"Don't worry. It's our mission to be the greatest puppy-sitters ever!" Bingo nudges Mr. Mousey toward Baby. She sniffs it and gives it a lick, and in three seconds, Mr. Mousey is completely covered in slobber.

Rolly realizes they have to find something else for Baby to do before the living room gets completely ruined. "I know what I always want to do: eat!"

The pups lead Baby into the kitchen and offer her the small teacup of food they had prepared. But Baby devours her food in one bite . . . and then finishes Bingo's and Rolly's bowls, too!

Bingo and Rolly decide to teach Baby some tricks in the backyard.

Bingo picks up a stick. "This is called 'fetch.' I throw the stick, and Rolly brings it back." Bingo throws the stick across the yard.

"Ta-da!" Rolly drops it in front of Baby. "Now it's your turn, Baby! Bring back the stick!"

Bingo picks up the stick again and throws it. "Not even Baby can make a mess of playing fetch in the backyard."

Or can she?

Instead of fetching the stick, Baby comes back with an entire tree in her mouth!

Rolly looks at his brother. "If we stay here, Baby might destroy the whole yard!"

"Then I think really great puppy-sitters would take a puppy to the dog park. Let's go!" Bingo says.

At the dog park, Baby runs around excitedly as Bingo and Rolly show her all the neat stuff there is to do.

But suddenly, the pups see something flying through the air.

"Stick!" they yell. Bingo and Rolly take off after it.

Baby starts to follow them, but then she hears a squeak and runs in the opposite direction!

Across the park, Baby had spotted a squeaky stuffed toy and ran over to play with it! But the squeaky toy belongs to Cupcake. "What's the big idea? That's mine!"

Cupcake grabs the other end of the toy and pulls. Baby playfully tugs back . . . until Cupcake narrows her eyes and growls.

Baby quickly lets go.

Meanwhile, the pups realize Baby is gone! They look all around the dog park, but Baby is nowhere to be seen.

Cupcake walks over to them. "Are you looking for that big drooly puppy that tried to take my toy before she ran outta here?"

Rolly nods and asks, "Which way did she go?"

Cupcake just shakes her head. "Only you two could lose the biggest puppy in the dog park."

Then it occurs to Bingo. "She *is* the biggest! Rolly, we just have to follow the biggest paw prints."

Rolly looks down and spots a large paw print in the dirt. "Like this one?" he asks.

"Exactly like that one!" Bingo says.

Bingo and Rolly follow the paw prints out of the park. Then they follow the prints and slobber through the neighborhood until they realize they are headed straight for their house.

Back at the house, the pups are delighted to find Hissy playing fetch with Baby and Mr. Mousey.

"I've got to admit, it is kind of fun to have a puppy around the house to play this game with again," Hissy tells her brothers.

Rolly grins. "You know, we're still puppies, too."

"I mean," Bingo adds, "we're still a *little* bit little."

Hissy shrugs. "Then get in this game! There's room for two more."

Later, when Bob gets home, the house is quiet. He finds all the animals snuggled up together.

Bob smiles at Bingo and Rolly. "Wow! The puppy really tuckered you out, huh?" Bingo and Rolly sleepily open their eyes. "Looks like you guys ended up being great puppy-sitters."

MISSION ACCOMPLISHED!

Father's Day Countdown

Bingo and Rolly are visiting their friend Keia at her doghouse for a day of fun. They are in her craft room when they decide to try out their flying machines. The pups are hooked up and ready to go when . . . *crash!*

They end up completely tangled in the yarn.

"How bad is it, Keia?" Bingo asks nervously.

"Looks preeetty tangly," she responds.

"Nothing's too tangly for Keia, master untangler!" Rolly says.

"Hmmm . . . let's see. Over, then under," Keia says to herself, concentrating.

Luckily, Keia does manage to untie them. They wiggle free and the three pups race to the yard to find Chloe.

"Hey, you guys!" Chloe says excitedly, doing a pirouette. "Check out my shoes! It's Father's Day, and my daddy's flying home from a business trip in Saint Louis just in time to take me to a father-daughter dance!" She can hardly wait for her dad to get home.

Just then, her mom comes out, holding her cell phone. Chloe's dad is on the line.

Chloe runs to the phone to talk to her dad. "Happy Father's Day, Daddy!" she says. "Are you at the airport?"

"Bad news, Chloe-bear . . ." her dad begins. "The plane's broken, so I may not make it to the dance. I'm so sorry. I love you."

After they hang up, Chloe turns to her mom with tears in her eyes. "I wish Daddy could get home for the dance."

"Me too," her mom says. "Maybe someone will fix the plane in time."

As soon as Chloe and her mom head inside, the pups decide to come up with a plan.

"We gotta go to Saint Louis to—" Bingo says.

"Fix the plane so Chloe's dad can get to the dance!" Keia finishes.

"Wait for me!" Cagey calls to them. "There's only one thing I love more than this wheel, and that's our Chloe. I want in on this mission!"

The pets all head to the airport to find a plane to Saint Louis. When they get there, they spot Frank and Esther.

"Hustle it, Frank! We gotta catch the plane to Saint Louis!" Esther says.

"That's our ride!" Bingo cheers. "C'mon!"

When they get to the gate, a flight attendant tells Frank and Esther that they've *just* missed the plane. "I'm so sorry," the flight attendant says. "You could take the high-speed train instead."

"You heard the lady," Bingo says. "We're taking a train."

"Planes and trains? Ooh! Missions are somethin' else!" says Cagey. "Hey, what's a train?"

Cagey and the pups take the train across the country to Saint Louis. They know they'll need a little luck to get there and bring Chloe's dad back in time for the father-daughter dance.

When the train stops in Saint Louis, the pets hop off with Frank and Esther.

"Which way to Chloe's dad's airport?" Keia asks the pups.

"I dunno," Bingo says.

Suddenly, something catches Bingo's eye. High above, a blimp drifts lazily back and forth.

"We should be able to see Chloe's dad's airport from up there!" says Bingo.

So Bingo, Rolly, and Keia activate their collars, and their helmets and harnesses deploy. Keia then puts a tiny harness on Cagey. They strap in and send their grappling hooks way up to the blimp.

Once they're safely in the blimp, they peer through the blimp door, searching and searching and searching for the . . .

"Airport! There!" Rolly shouts.

"Now we just need to get down there," Rolly says.

"Let's parachute!" Bingo suggests. "Ready, set, jump!"

They push buttons on their collars again, and parachutes deploy.

The pets float down, landing in a heap on a spot of grass near the airport's tarmac.

From the pile, Rolly pulls out a little round gear he was sitting on.

Just then, an airport worker says something about the plane missing a part.

"You found it, Rolly!" says Bingo. "If we can figure out where that gear goes, maybe that will fix the plane."

With the gear, they rush up the stairs to the plane. A tangle of wires pops out from a compartment, covering the space for the missing gear.

"Whoa!" Keia gasps. "That's a lot of wires."

"You're the master untangler, remember?" Rolly adds.

"I believe in you, Sis!" Cagey says. "For Chloe!"

Keia beams and then gets to work, determined to fix the plane.

Keia works quickly to untangle the wires. She clears the way and then clicks the gear into place. The engines fire up! She did it!

"Now Chloe's dad can make it home for the dance," Rolly says.

"And we can make it home if we take the plane, too," says Bingo.

The pets all head inside the airport to search for Chloe's dad. They spot him walking *away* from the gate. He's going to miss the plane unless they find a way to let him know it's taking off soon!

The four friends quickly form a plan. Cagey takes hold of the handle on Chloe's dad's suitcase while Bingo, Rolly, and Keia roll it toward the gate.

Chloe's dad runs after it. The plan is working!

Chloe's dad catches up to his suitcase as he gets to the gate. "I thought the plane was broken!" he says to an airport worker.

"The plane is fixed now and ready for takeoff," the airport worker tells him.

"Yes! He's getting on the plane!" Keia says.

"And so should we!" Rolly reminds them.

When they're back at Keia's house, they run through the doggie door and into the kitchen to find Chloe.

"Wow, look at those dancing shoes!" Chloe's dad says.

"Daddy! You're here!" Chloe cries, running to him for a big hug. "Happy Father's Day, Daddy!"

"I like this whole mission thing," Cagey tells the pups.

MISSION ACCOMPLISHED!

ICe, ICe, PUGGY

After mowing the lawn, Bob comes inside and heads into the kitchen for a glass of iced tea before work.

"Oh, no!" Bob says when he opens the freezer door. "I'm all out of ice! How's a guy supposed to have iced tea if he doesn't have any ice?"

Disappointed, Bob sets the ice tray on the counter and then heads off to work.

"I wish we knew where to get Bob the ice he needs for iced tea," Bingo says to Rolly.

"A.R.F. can show you!" A.R.F. barks. He knows exactly where to find the best ice. He projects an image of Antarctica.

"Cool!" Rolly cheers.

"It's more than cool," A.R.F. says. "It's *cold*."

"Doesn't matter," Bingo replies. "If it's got what Bob needs, then Rolly and I need to be there. Come on, Rolly. You and I are going on a mission!"

The pups hurry through the doggie door and race to the airport to board a cargo plane heading to Antarctica.

ANTARCTICA

TO: SOUTH POLE

VIA AIR

When they make it to Antarctica, they aren't sure where to look for the best ice, but they see some penguins who might be able to help.

"What are you two doggies doing here?" Mr. Penguin asks.

"We're on a mission, looking for ice," Bingo tells him.

The penguin agrees to find the pups the very best ice if they'll watch his egg while he looks.

So Mr. Penguin waddles off to look for ice, and the pups watch the egg.

They put the egg on a piece of wood, and Bingo even places a ski hat on top of it.

"There!" Bingo exclaims. "Off the ice and toasty warm."

Suddenly, the wind blows the egg away!

Bingo and Rolly slip, slide, and tumble after it.

"We can't let it get away!" Bingo calls to his brother.

The egg and the pups slide right into a cave.

When the pups catch up to the egg, it's in two broken pieces.

"I don't remember Mr. Penguin's egg being broken when we followed it in here," Rolly says.

"Because it wasn't . . ." Bingo replies. The ski hat that had been keeping the egg warm is now moving. Bingo goes to investigate and lifts up the hat. "It's a baby penguin!"

"We should go looking for her dad," Rolly says,
"so we can show him his new daughter."

"Yeah! And we can see if he found Bob's ice," Bingo adds.

But the walls begin to crack! Huge icicles fall all around them. The cave is filling up with icicles that form an icy maze.

"I hope we're not trapped in here!" Rolly shouts.

The pups run this way and that way until they eventually make their way out.

When they catch up to the baby penguin, they end up on slippery ice. They slip and slide around until they're by her side.

Then they hear a *crack*! The ice under them breaks off and they start to float away.

"We'll be okay as long as we stick together," Bingo assures the baby penguin and Rolly.

But then the ice starts to sink.

"What are we gonna do?" Rolly asks, worried.

Then they hear a voice.

It's Mr. Penguin! He helps the pups float to the mainland.

"Do you have my egg?" he asks when they get there.

The baby penguin waddles off the ice chunk and hugs her dad. "Da-da!" she says.

"My little girl!" says Mr. Penguin with a huge smile.

Mr. Penguin thanks the pups for taking care of his egg and
tells them that the very ice they're standing on is the best in all of
Antarctica. He helps them break it up into cubes, and Bingo and
Rolly put the ice in their collars to take home for Bob.

"So long, baby penguin," Bingo says.

"We'd love to stay here and play with you, but my brother and I
have to get home as fast as we can!" Rolly adds.

They wave goodbye to their new friends and head for home.

When Bob gets back from work, his glass is full of ice.

"Wait a minute. . . . There's ice in this glass? This is perfect for the iced tea I've been wanting all day!" Bob says as he gets the pitcher of tea from the refrigerator.

Bingo and Rolly smile at each other.

MISSION ACCOMPLISHED!

ADOPT-a-PaLOOZa

It's Adopt-a-palooza, the day for pets who need people and people who need pets to come together and make forever families. Bob is volunteering. Bingo, Rolly, and Keia are helping, too!

"This is where Chloe's family met me," Keia says.

Bingo leaps after a ball. But another dog leaps even higher!

"Bow to the wow!" Bingo says. "Nice catch!"

"Thanks! I'm Lollie," the pup replies. His mom is also a volunteer.

Rolly darts over to the puppy playpen.

"Baby puppies!" he coos. "They're so cute and tiny!"

"I bet every one of these puppies will find a home today," Keia says.

"Except for the one who ran away," Cupcake adds.

Cupcake points to a tunnel in the dirt. A puppy escaped so he could chase after a squirrel!

"Oh, no!" Rolly cries.

Keia is worried. If the puppy doesn't get back soon, he'll miss his chance to find a family!

"It looks like we have our mission," Bingo says. "A puppy-finding mission!"

Rolly will stay behind to be the puppy-sitter. "Uncle Rolly's here!" he tells the cuddly crew.

"We should go talk to the squirrels in the park," Bingo tells Lollie and Keia. "Maybe one of them knows which squirrel the puppy was chasing!"

Bingo and Keia activate their collars. Hang gliders pop out.

"Whoa!" Lollie gasps. "So cool!"

Keia buckles her new friend in tightly. These puppies are ready to fly!

The puppies soar
into the treetops.
They push
through piles of acorns.

They nudge
through nests.
They find
plenty of squirrels.

But not a single
one will talk to them.
Every time the puppies
get close, the squirrels
run away.

Keia, Bingo, and Lollie head back to Adopt-a-palooza.

"All those squirrels are too scared of puppies to talk to us," Keia says.

"Too bad you can't ask the squirrel who lives in Keia's yard," Rolly says. "He always plays with us."

"We should go to Keia's yard and talk to that squirrel!" Lollie suggests.

"Follow me!" Keia says, leading the way.

A few minutes later, they find the squirrel—and the little lost puppy!

"We've got to get you back to the park so you can find a family!" Bingo tells the pup.

The puppy starts to follow them toward the gate, but he gets distracted by Keia's doghouse and runs inside.

"No!" the friends shout. "Stay with us!"

Bingo chases after him. "Puppy, sit!" he yells.

Just when Bingo gets hold of the puppy, he wiggles away.

"I'll get him, Bingo!" Keia calls.

The puppy rushes into Keia's craft room.

Keia finds him in a pile of fabric scraps and pipe cleaners.

Just when Keia thinks she can get ahold of the puppy, he scampers away.

"I'll get him, Keia!" Lollie calls.

Lollie finds the puppy chowing down on some tasty dog treats.

"He's here!" Lollie calls to his friends. "Now how do we get him back to the park?"

"He really likes those snacks," Bingo observes. "Maybe he'll follow a trail of treats!"

There's just one problem: Keia doesn't have enough treats to make a trail all the way to the dog park.

"I wish that squirrel would run back to the dog park," Lollie says. "Then the puppy would chase him again."

"Lollie, that's brilliant!" Bingo cheers.

"I don't think the squirrel will agree," Lollie says.

"We don't need that squirrel," Keia says.

Bingo and Lollie follow Keia up to her craft room.

SNIP! SNIP! SNIP!

Keia whips up three squirrel costumes.

When the puppy sees the three new "squirrels," he begins to bark.

Bingo, Lollie, and Keia run to the dog park!

Bingo, Lollie, and Keia run down the sidewalk.
The puppy follows them.

Bingo, Lollie, and Keia hop from car to car on the miniature train.
The puppy follows them.

Bingo, Lollie, and Kcia slip
down the slide in the playground.
The puppy follows them.

Finally, the little puppy is back where he belongs.

A little boy walks up to the playpen with his mother.

"Mom, look!" the boys says. "That funny puppy has some fabric stuck in his collar. Is that your cape? Are you a little superhero?" the boy says with a giggle. "Mom, can we adopt this one? We can name him Hero!"

"Okay," the mom agrees. "He does seem sweet and calm."

And that's how little Hero got his name and his forever home.

MISSION ACCOMPLISHED!

BiNGO aND ROLLY'S BiRTHDAY

Today is a very special day. The sun is shining, birds are singing, and Bob is sleeping—until Bingo and Rolly leap onto his bed and start to bounce.

"Hooray, it's birthday day!" Rolly shouts.

"Happy birthday, fellas!" Bob lets out a big yawn. "Why don't you play outside until I'm done sleeping?"

The pups run out, laughing all the way. This is going to be the best puppy birthday ever!

Rolly heads straight for his favorite thing in the backyard: a gigantic stack of sticks. "Now that I'm a year older, I'm going to make my stick collection even bigger!" But when he goes to add a new stick to his pile, it topples to the ground. "I wish my sticks would stop spilling everywhere. . . ."

Across the yard, Bingo is playing his favorite game: launching his Captain Dog action figure. He puts the toy into the launcher and hits a button. *BOING!* After chasing after it, Bingo reloads the launcher. "Captain Dog to the rescue!" But the spring snaps and Captain Dog goes nowhere. "No! It's broken!" Bingo cries.

"Who's ready for their breakfast birthday bones?" Bob calls.
Bingo and Rolly run inside, thinking breakfast will cheer them up.
Bob promises them a puppy party later. "I made you each a
present. See you tonight!" he says as he leaves for work.

"So, what gifts did you get for each other?" Hissy asks.

Bingo and Rolly are confused. Bob said *he* was giving them presents.

"Don't you want to give something to each other?" Hissy asks.

The puppies exchange looks.

"I want you to have the best birthday ever!" Bingo says to Rolly.

"Ditto!" Rolly replies with his mouth full.

"C'mon, Rolly! We'd better start our gift mission," Bingo says.

Bingo thinks he has found the perfect gift. He runs inside and drops it at Hissy's feet. "I got Rolly a stick from his stick collection," Bingo says.

Hissy laughs. "Why don't you think about something Rolly *doesn't* have?" Bingo thinks for a moment, then remembers what Rolly said earlier. "A stick holder!" Bingo exclaims. He runs off.

Then Rolly comes in with a gift. Hissy laughs again. "That's Bingo's toy," she says.

"That's how I know he'll like it!" Rolly replies.

"What would he like that he doesn't have already?" Hissy asks.

"He used to like launching his Captain Dog fetch toy," Rolly says.

"Maybe I can find him something springy!" Rolly dashes out the front door.

Rolly goes to visit their friend Dallie the firehouse Dalmatian. "That spring! It's just what I'm looking for!" Rolly exclaims.

"I'd give it to you, but I need it to prop up the front of my doghouse," Dallie says. "If you've got something else that can get the job done, I'd be happy to trade you."

So Rolly decides to trade his stick collection for Dallie's spring.

"Seems like you really love those sticks, though," says Dallie.

"Yeah," Rolly says, "I do. But not as much as I love my brother! See ya, Dallie. I've got a present to wrap!"

At the dog park, Bingo spots Cupcake and Rufus playing with a box that would be perfect for Rolly's stick collection. He asks if he can give it to Rolly.

"You're barking up the wrong tree," Cupcake says. "Unless . . . you want to trade me something better."

Bingo brings all his favorite toys to Cupcake and Rufus. Cupcake spots Bingo's Captain Dog action figure. "That's the one I want!"

Bingo sighs. "Okay," he says. "For Rolly, I'll trade. He's going to be so excited to see this box!"

The pups bring their presents to the middle of the backyard. "Open yours first!" Bingo shouts.

"No, you go first!" Rolly says.

The brothers open their presents at the same time. "It's a spring to launch your Captain Dog action figure," Rolly says excitedly when Bingo opens his present.

"And yours is a stick holder, for your stick collection!" says Bingo.

"What are you waiting for?" Bingo asks. "Put your sticks in there!"

"The thing is . . . I don't have them anymore. I traded my stick collection to Dallie for that spring," Rolly says. "So let's use it to launch Captain Dog!"

"We can't. . . . I traded Captain Dog to Cupcake for your present," Bingo tells his brother.

"Aren't you sad you can't play with your toys?" Hissy asks.

"Yeah," Bingo says. "But I have a brother who traded his most favorite thing just to make me happy."

"And that's better than any present I can think of," Rolly adds.

A.R.F. thinks this is lovely. "A.R.F. is having big feelings!" he cries.

When Bob gets home, he calls the puppies into the house. "Who's ready for a birthday party?" Bob gives them sweaters he knitted himself.

"We love 'em, Bob!" Bingo says.

"Thank you so much!" Rolly jumps up and down.

Bingo and Rolly's birthday is almost over. But they still have two more presents from Hissy that are waiting in the backyard.

"My stick collection!" Rolly shouts.

"And my Captain Dog! How did you get our stuff back?" Bingo asks.

"I just made a couple of trades," Hissy replies.

Bingo and Rolly give her big puppy hugs. "You're the best kitty sister in the whole world!" Rolly says.

"I know," Hissy says with a smile. "Don't rub it in."

Rolly's stick collection fits perfectly in his new box.

Bingo uses the new spring in his toy launcher and makes the Captain Dog figure fly through the air. "And Captain Dog flies again!" he shouts excitedly.

Hissy watches them play. "Happy birthday, Brothers!"

MISSION ACCOMPLISHED!